The Winter Visitors

by Karel Hayes

For my husband and son, Brent and John Gorey

ISBN 978-0-89272-750-6

Printed in China

5   4   3

Down East Books
Camden, Maine
A division of Down East Enterprise
Book Orders: 800-685-7962
www.downeastbooks.com
Distributed to the trade by National Book Network

Library of Congress Cataloging-in-Publication Data:
Hayes, Karel. 1949-
  The winter visitors / by Karel Hayes.
     p. cm.
  Summary: When the summer visitors leave in the fall, a
new group of visitors moves into the vacation cottage to
spend the winter.
  ISBN 978-0-89272-750-6 (trade hardcover : alk. paper)
[1. Bears--Fiction. 2. Winter--Fiction.] I. Title.
PZ7.H31476Win 2007
[E]--dc22
                                              2007014051

In the fall

the summer visitors will be going,

going,

gone.

Then the winter visitors will come

to stay,

and play,

and have a New Year's party.

Afterward, they'll have a rest

until winter snow stops falling.

Then, in the spring, they will be going,

going,

gone.

And when the summer visitors return,

they will not know

what went on

while they were gone.